60 Mound Street

By Judith Toombs Gatch

Illustrated By Ann Gatch

ISBN: 061595698X
ISBN-13: 978-0615956985

DEDICATION

I wish to dedicate this book to Daniel, Lillianna, and Clairissa, who are the heart, the soul, and the spirit of my existence.

CONTENTS

ACKNOWLEDGMENTS

I wish to thank Ann Gatch, Jennifer Reges, and Mary Rutledge for their help, advice, and support in the completion of this book. I also wish to thank Chris Cheney for his graphic design help.

60 Mound Street

Chapter 1
The Immigrant

I will get caught someday. That is a given. I have decided to write down how I happened to be here. I'm doing this so that there will be a record of my intentions, should I happen to be found out. I am also writing because it fills up my quiet time, and because I like using my words on paper. I didn't wake up that scorching, sidewalk baking September day with disappearing in mind. If that had been in my mind, I would have had a plan. I would have taken my other shirt or something. I was awake until three in the morning the night before. My bed was on the floor in the living room of our third floor apartment. Sleeping in the living room was okay with me because there was a window and a breeze to help cool off these scorching hot nights.

Dad slinked in late that night, drunk as usual. I pretended to be asleep because he was always looking for a fight when he was drinking. Morning came too soon. I awoke with Mom yelling she'd be late for work. My little sister was crying, but she is always crying. Dad kicked me in the leg and yelled, "Get up sissy boy!" Our bathroom was down the hall, and my sister got there first. She called me a string of dirty words when I asked her to hurry up. She can thank Dad for teaching her the dirty words. After a while, she emerged, and I got a turn. It wasn't much of a bathroom. There was a sink with a thin stream of cold water, a toilet, and a broken shower. Suddenly, there was a lot of screaming. Dad was yelling and sister was crying. I ran to the bedroom door and realized Dad was trying to shave off her long hair. "I told you if you brought cooties into this house one more time, I'd shave you bald! I have been bitten for the last time." My sister was terrified. It is true that he did say that. But it was the first day of school, and little girls need their hair. Do you realize the hell she would go through if he succeeded?

"Stop!" I shouted. "Leave her alone!" This really made Dad mad. He let go of her and grabbed me.

"Run," I shouted, and boy did she take off!

I knew she understood the drill. She could go to school, see the nurse, and they would treat her head. All I had to do was give her time to get out. I fought enough to give Dad a hard time. When I thought she had cleared the block, I just gave up. In a few minutes I was shaved as clean as a baby's butt. Some first day! Everyone would have new clothes, new school supplies, and I would have a shaven head, a wrinkled dirty T-shirt, and jeans cut off to look like shorts. If I was really lucky, I'd find a broken pencil somewhere, so I wouldn't get yelled at for not being prepared.

At this point, I headed for school. In my head, I had a plan. I would go to school, do what I had to do, and come back home. I would just ignore everyone. On my way to school, Mrs. Bea was on her stoop. This lady was the only person that was ever kind to me. Some boys had been throwing rocks at her little dog. I yelled at them to leave her alone, and they ran off. She was a nice person. She would let my mom use the phone sometimes, she gave my sister her daughter's old clothes that looked like new, and she gave me cookies almost every week. These cookies were not store bought cookies, but real homemade cookies with chocolate chips, or oatmeal with raisins. Her nut bread was really awesome. She yelled to me to stop. "Hey, come here. I got you some oatmeal cookies." I'd walk a hundred miles for them. As I turned to leave, she handed me a can of soda. "You can have it for lunch," she said. Bald or not, just maybe, this day would be okay.

I should have known better than to hope for a good day. I ate the cookies as fast as I could, before anyone could take them away from me. They were heaven! I'm glad I did, because when I walked into the classroom, the soda fell out of my pocket and rolled across the floor. The teacher put his big ol' foot on it and snapped out something about me gobbling up a free lunch everyday paid for by his tax dollars, and spending my money on crap like soda. He was always saying stuff like that to me. "I have a pool. You want a pool? You have to be like me. I have a nice car. You want a nice car? You have to be like me." That fool! I will never be like him. Never! If I starve to death tomorrow, I will not be like him. The rest of the class felt the same way. They made fun of him all the time. I noticed that the heaviness was once more on my heart. I felt like I was in a deep well and every time I tried to pull myself out, someone would step on my fingers. The heaviness felt like a brick pushing down hard on my heart.

We had math, then music, then social studies. I always liked social studies, because teachers never taught it. They showed films, or had us read the book. I liked that. We had a film about how hard it was for immigrants to leave their homes and start a new life in a foreign land. They wanted peace, freedom, and to love GOD the way they wanted. I started thinking about that. It wouldn't be hard for me to just up and leave. I'd do it and not for all that goodie goodie stuff either. I'd do it just so I'd never have to deal with these people again. I'd do it, so I could wake up feeling good and go to bed feeling good. I must have drifted off in my own world, because the next thing I knew, the teacher was yelling at me. He said I'd have to stay after school and make up the time I wasted by dreaming. I nodded, and we were dismissed for lunch. I didn't eat lunch. The thought of that jerk paying for it with his tax dollars turned my stomach. I had been here half a day and no kid had talked to me. I can't blame them. I look pretty much a mess. After lunch, we had an assembly. You know the kind they have on the first day. All the classes show up, and then they yell at you about growing up to be bums if you don't get educated. My class sat in the back. I could hardly sit there. They talked on and on, but it just sounded garbled to me. I stopped understanding their words. In my head, I kept thinking about those immigrants. My heart raced! I just couldn't sit there any longer.

I'm not usually a troublemaker or a school goof off, so when I asked to go to the restroom, the monitor let me go. I walked out of the auditorium and used the restroom. I put cold water on my face. I couldn't make myself go back inside. I walked past the office. I walked out the front door. I walked off the school grounds. No one spoke to me or tried to stop me. I was invisible.

I kept walking until I was in the heart of Cincinnati. I had almost two dollars in my pocket that I had saved all summer. I looked over a line of Metro Buses. Something in my head said to get on #28, so I did. I asked the driver where the end of the line was. He said that would be Milford, Ohio, about seventeen miles East of Cincinnati. Now, that isn't exactly a new frontier, but it is farther than I had ever been.

The bus was quiet. It was also air-conditioned. I thought people wouldn't sit by me because of the way I looked. I wondered if I smelled bad. A lady sat down by me who was round all over. Her face was round and her cheeks were red. Her body was round and she had teeny, tiny feet. She even smiled at me. I sat back and felt like a rich man going home from work. I knew I should be scared, but I wasn't. The sky was so blue, and here and there was a white, puffy cloud floating ever so slowly across the sky. The trip followed the river, the Ohio River. I really felt a calm peacefulness. The lady sitting next to me reached in her bag and took out a candy bar. It was a Snickers. Then she took out a second one and handed it to me. She just smiled and pushed the candy into my hand. I'm two seconds from the city and already people are nicer. I began to see houses with big, green lawns. Kids were riding bikes without grownups around. There were dogs running with the kids, not attacking them. I saw a Milford City sign and everyone stood up to get off. I followed, just like I knew where I was going. Milford was going to be my new home in the wilderness. I had reached my new frontier. I was thinking things like, "Will I have to fight off Indians, kill a bear for food, or sleep in a cave full of bats?" I know that was silly, but that was how my mind was going.

I stood on the sidewalk until I saw a bench in front of a barbershop. Can you believe it that barbershop had one of those red and white poles like you see in the cowboy movies? I sat on the bench to warm up from the air-conditioned bus. I picked a street that had the most green grass and trees and decided to walk in that direction. There were three boys bouncing a basketball. When they caught up to me, they asked if I wanted to play ball. They said I would round out the team. I said I wasn't very good. They replied that they weren't either, that they just played for fun. They had a slab of concrete and a net right in their backyard. Can you believe that? They were nice guys. We shot hoops for a long time. Then one of the guy's sister came out with popsicles for everyone. She said "Hi! I'm Clairissa, wanna popsicle?" She didn't even make me pay. Well, these certainly were not wild Indians. The lady called to them to come to dinner. Everyone began to go inside. The alley ran behind the boys' yard.

It was time for me to find that cave to sleep in for the night. This alley wasn't like downtown alleys. There were trashcans but no garbage around them. Some yards were fenced. Flowers and big trees grew everywhere. Dogs ran up to the fence barking to be petted but not to attack you. You could look at a house and tell if they had kids by the bicycles, plastic dollhouses, swings, sandboxes, jungle gyms, and other stuff they had in the yard. Nobody seemed to be worried about people stealing any of it. In the middle of all this was a little white house with a rusty back gate. The roof was pointy on top and there were big trees all around it. A car came up the alley and stopped at that gate. Then a man got out and opened the back door of the house to let out the dog. After that, he did the strangest thing. He got back in his car and drove off leaving the dog out and the back door open.

I don't know what made me do it, but I jumped the fence, petted that dog and walked in the back door. You could see straight through the house, out the kitchen, out the dining room, right out to the street. I was shocked to see that in front of the house was the same man getting out of his parked car. I don't know why I didn't run back to the alley. But I didn't. I ran down the basement steps instead. WOW! There was the biggest bunch of trains I'd ever seen. In one corner was a stack of old furniture like tables, chairs, old dressers and trunks. You know, stuff like they had in the old days. It was all dusty, so I knew they didn't use that corner much. As quickly as I could move, I wiggled myself under that furniture as far back from view as I could scoot. Then I just laid there waiting for my heart beat to slow down. I had to pee something awful, but I didn't move. I heard a lady come home and smelled food cooking. I was too scared to be hungry. The man spent most of the evening in the basement playing with the train. At ten, he locked up the house and they both went to bed. I couldn't believe how dark it was. I really was too tired to worry. I would have to wait until tomorrow to get out anyway. I fell asleep almost at once.

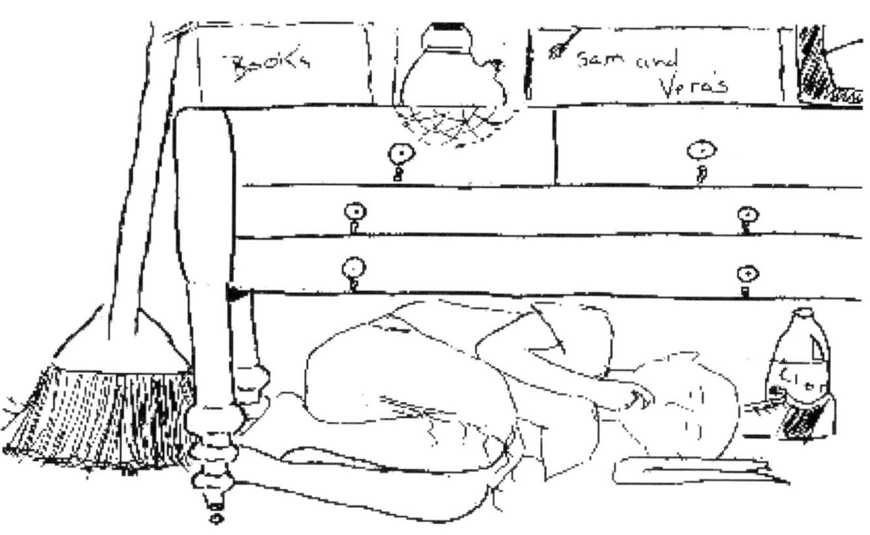

Chapter 2
The Making Of My Own Home

I awoke in the morning as the man readied for work. I knew the woman was in the house somewhere, so I didn't move. She left about seven-thirty. I was relieved to know that at last, I was alone. I had planned to leave first thing, but during the night, it began to rain really hard. Now it was pouring. I went up the basement steps, stopping to listen on each step. I saw the dog up there at the top, wagging her tail. I always wanted a dog. This dog had red hair and was rather bedraggled. I don't know why anyone would choose this dog, but then I was a misfit too. I figured we belonged together. I talked to her. I let her smell my hand. She just wagged her tail. I figured she would bark if anyone came close. She was my own personal alarm system.

I found the bathroom. Boy, did I have to go! There was a bathtub and clean towels and two kinds of soap and three kinds of shampoo and lotion. I just couldn't resist. I only had taken showers. I always wanted a sit down bath. Before I knew what I was doing, I was sitting in a tub of hot water soaking every part of my body. After a while, it dawned on me that I would have to clean the bathtub really good, so no one would know I had been there. When I climbed out, I did just that. I gathered up my clothes and the towel and went back to the basement and put them in a washer. Can you believe having a washer-dryer right in your house that you don't have to put quarters in? I was glad I had been doing the laundry for Mom since I was eight. I knew what to do. I was clean. I was going to have clean clothes. I had to wait for the clothes to dry. That is when I realized I was very hungry.

I looked in the refrigerator. There was leftover spaghetti. I took a plate and helped myself. I put it in the microwave. I took a Coke too. I was in heaven. They had orange juice in a cute pitcher like the Cosby's do on TV. This was the best breakfast I had ever had. I was having it in a stranger's house with no clothes and only a dog for company.

I washed up the kitchen and put everything back in its place. Then I checked out the house. There were two bedrooms. One was used for sleeping. The other had a computer and a bunch of books. It looked like a teacher lived here, because there were teacher manuals everywhere along with colored paper and markers. There was a living room and a big dining room. The place had a large front porch with flowers that made the house welcoming. While I waited for my clothes to dry, I got to thinking. This was the best I had ever had it. These folks didn't know I was there. What would it matter if I stayed a while? Who would care?

I put on my dry clothes and looked around the basement. If I was going to stay, I needed to make my place under the furniture more comfortable. In a bag marked "Goodwill," I found an old, torn sleeping bag. I dragged it under the furniture. I rolled up a bunch of old towels for a pillow. They had about eighteen empty Clorox bottles stored. Who would keep eighteen of those? I decided it would be good to have one to pee in. I took another to put clean water in, in case I got thirsty. I felt like that bird outside the school window that built her nest for spring. I, too, was building a nest. After making sure my nest was comfortable, I went back to the kitchen. I packed two peanut butter and jelly sandwiches and put them in a bag. I put in an apple and five cookies. These were store bought. I didn't even know what kind they were. I had to stop myself from being greedy. If I took another Coke, they would probably miss it. I once again cleaned the kitchen. I stored my dinner in the nest.

Now, my needs were met, I explored once again. I could tell from the pictures that they had two grown daughters. One, I think, was married with a kid. I know because there was a picture of them on the wall. I wasn't going to worry about them, because they probably lived far away. I also found a big white cat. He spent most of the day hiding from me. I had no idea when these people would come home. Honestly I didn't think about it, until I heard a car door slam. I looked at the clock. It was four-thirty. I ran for the basement and crawled into my nest, just as the front door opened.

About five, the lady came in. They don't scream or cuss or

anything. Their conversation went like this:

"I thought we had more spaghetti."

"Well, maybe Meg stopped in and got hungry."

"Do you want baked fish tomorrow?"

"Sure, why not."

"Penny sure is tired today. She didn't want to walk when I got home."

"Maybe she played with Daniel when Meg stopped by."

AH HA! I now knew three things. They had a girl named Meg with a baby named Daniel who lived close enough to drop by. And the dog's name was Penny. I ate my wonderful sandwiches and got warm in my bed. My first day in my nest had been wonderful. I hoped I'd never have to leave.

Day two: I had Cheerio's with a banana on top. I had orange juice. I had thought, in the night, that I should look for a hiding place upstairs in case someone comes and I can't make it to the basement. While I was waiting for the computer to come on, I looked the house over. There was a skinny bed in the computer room, with a spread that hung to the floor. There were boxes of books and stuff underneath. If I crawled under there and pushed the boxes forward, I could get behind them. That would be nest number two. I put a Clorox bottle under there and a tattered blanket and a ragged pillow. I had two rather comfortable nests. I collected little things that might be fun to do at night. I found a flashlight, extra batteries, a joke book, and a book about snakes in South America, a deck of cards, and some colored paper. All this was dragged to my nest and concealed inside a wooden box that sat up on legs. It had a sticker on it that said, "Aunt Mildred's hope chest." I wonder what she was hoping.

Then I turned my attention to the computer. There were all kinds of math games. I had a great time and I didn't have to share. There was one called pre-algebra. I didn't think I was smart enough to do that one. It had an example and in no time I was climbing up the levels. I took a paper notebook, pencils, and markers to my basement nest. I do get bored in the evening. I took a big, old, heavy book to use as a table. What a happy home I had! I had been two days in this house and one day getting here. I wonder if anyone missed me. I'm betting NOT! Tomorrow I'll check the news.

Day three, then day four, and no news about me. I didn't expect there to be. I am invisible. I was living high on the hog. I hadn't been kicked, slapped, yelled at, or put down in five days. If they do find me, I'll run off again.

At noon on day five, I turned on the news. There was a report of a boy gone missing. It was me. The newsperson said I hadn't returned home from school the day before. My dad was there looking sad, saying he waited and waited for me to come home, but I didn't. My mother was yelling that she wanted her son back. But she always yells. My sister said I had been gone since the first day of school. She cried. But she always cries. The school principal said he had checked attendance and that I had been in school for the past four days. (Well, I guess we know how good their records are.) The thing that just about broke my heart was an interview with Mrs. Bea. She told them with tears on her face that she saw me the first day of school and not after that day. She assured them that I had been missing since then. They didn't believe her. They took the word of my dad and that jerk at the school. They went on to say no one had spotted me anywhere. Then they showed a picture of me from two years ago with hair down over my eyes. No wonder no one recognized me. Dad hadn't told Mom that he shaved my head. My sister had run off, so she didn't know either. No wonder no one saw me. The lady on the bus didn't see me. The boys that I shot hoops with didn't see me. I was invisible.

I felt bad about Mrs. Bea. I had to let her know I was okay. How could I do that without giving away my hiding place? I decided to call when I knew she was at church and leave a message on her answering machine. If it was short, they probably couldn't trace the call. That is what I did. I called and said, "Mrs. Bea, don't worry about me. I wasn't kidnapped. I'm not with any gang. I'm happy. I love your cookies. I miss you." Then I hung up the phone. I hoped she would understand. I could almost hear what people were thinking.

DAD

The damn kids make so much noise in this poop-covered apartment, I just wanted to scream. I sent that prancy ass son of mine out to tend to the trash and yelled for my little girl to hurry up. That's when I noticed her clawing at her head. I knew it! Once more she was hoppin' with head lice. I warned her. I warned all of them. One more case of cooties and I'd shave them bald! Shaving is what my dad did to me. It cured them for a time.

I grabbed her skinny little arm and lifted her on the stool. She was a scrappy one. I'll say that. That's when that waste of a son of mine walked in. He is such a sneak. He waited until I reached for the razor and then lifted her off the stool. He told her to run, and she sure took off. Faster than lightening, she was out the door and gone. With that kind of fight in her, I know there is some of me in her blood.

That boy is another story. Little girl ran, but HE wasn't that quick. I grabbed his spindly arm and in a flash, I had him shaved bald. He didn't even fight. He just sat there and let me do it. What a waste of a kid. He will probably grow up to be a mamma's boy, 'cause he ain't ever gonna be like his ol' man. When I finished, he got up slowly and walked out. I ain't seen him since.

Candy Boy took off somewhere. Little girl says he's been gone four days. I don't believe her. She tends to lie. I know I saw him around here somewhere. But then, I've been busy. I got business to tend to, you know. I don't think anything happened to him. I don't think he was snatched. My old lady is pissed. She's cryin' all the time. She has to get a grip. She can't work in that shape. It's just not my fault.

TEACHER

You'd think these kids would clean up the first day of school, but look at that! It looks like he slept in those clothes. Wrinkled T-shirt! Dusty, torn shorts! No strings in his sneakers! The only thing new about him is his skinhead haircut. Well, I guess we know what he is taught at home.

I let him know when that "DEW" rolled across the floor that his spare money should be spent on food instead of soda. My tax dollars pay for his food, so he can sleep in class. I have to pay for my kids' food. We ought to just stop feeding these lazy ass kids. Send them out to clean the streets. I'd let them grow their own damn food. Well, he didn't open his mouth, but then he never did.

The office called for my attendance at the end of the day. Some kid is missing. I wasn't even sure which one it was. They asked me if he was here at dismissal. I just didn't remember him. The picture they showed me looked a little familiar but he looked too young to be in my class. I was not going to get in trouble for some kid that decided to take a powder. I just said, "Yea, he was in school.

He probably just ran off to be with his gang." His mother just looked at me with tears in her eyes. "I don't know why you would say that," is all she said. They all join gangs sooner or later. That's when I realized it was the bald kid with the "DEW."

MRS. BEA

He walks by many times a day, always alone, always with that far-a-way look in his eyes. Sometimes I give him cookies or some nut bread I've baked. He'd put some of it in his pocket. I asked him why one day. He said it was for his little sister.

I've heard the way they talk to him. The mother works hard, but she put a lot on that boy. She tried to turn him into the man of the house, because her husband sure wasn't. That was a lot to put on a boy that is that young and that frail. That father just yelled and cursed and put him down. I offered to watch the children for free while the mother worked. She said no because it would upset her husband. He don't allow charity.

Mr. All High and Mighty don't mind taken his wife's check the minute she got in the door for booze instead of tending to those poor kids. I guess all I can do is hand out cookies. I gave him a kind word when I could. But it just broke my heart when he'd walk by.

Now they say he ran off yesterday. I don't believe them. I haven't seen him since the first day of school. I've been waiting for him, because I made nut bread with black walnuts. That's his favorite. I don't know where he could be. "God, please, please watch over him!" I don't think I'll ever feel good again.

MOM

"God, PLEASE, PLEASE, watch over my son!"

Chapter 3

Paying My Way

I felt sure I was safe from discovery now. I passed my days in outstanding joy. I ate well and I was clean and free from the night terrors that happened when Dad came home drunk. I played on the computer. I got really good at the math games. I read a joke book and a book about an ugly dog called Beautiful Joe. That big book I took as a desktop turned out to be a teacher's manual for social studies. At first I would try a lesson and cheat. The answers were in the book. That got boring. Now I do them and then check the answers. You know it is fun to learn when you can also be the teacher. September passed in this manner.

One night when I couldn't sleep, I realized that I was really stealing from these people. Sure, they didn't miss anything, but in my heart, I knew I was stealing. If I was going to stay, and I knew I was, I had to find a way to pay them back. I drifted off to sleep wondering how I would do that. The next evening I heard Judy and Bill talking about the weekend. "I know what I'll be doing," said Bill, "I'll be raking the leaves."

That was it. That was a job I could do to pay for my living here. Now raking leaves was not as easy as it sounds. This house was surrounded by huge trees. I'd be surprised if the job could be done in one day. Raking them would easily pay for my September food. The next day was Friday. If I started when they left for work, I might be able to get them all raked. At least now, I had a plan.

As soon as Judy pulled off in her car, I was out the back door with a rake. I began at the back fence. I didn't see a single soul. I guess everyone out here worked. I had not done any exercise in a month. Every muscle quivered as I raked. I skipped lunch and kept right on going. By one-thirty, I was done. It was a good thing too.

There was an increase in cars on the road. I went inside, threw my clothes in the washer, jumped in the shower and let the hot water soak into all my muscles. I ate a grilled cheese, an apple, and a big glass of chocolate milk. I put my clothes in the dryer and watched a rerun of Gilligan's Island. I wiggled back into my clothes and crawled back into my nest. It was just in time too. Bill came home a half hour early. Man! My Guardian Angel was really on the job.

When Judy came home, I heard Bill say, "Did you hire someone to rake the leaves? You know I was going to do that."

"No," Judy replied. "Do you think one of the girls did that?"

I don't know what they decided because I was asleep. I had never been so tired. But it was a good tired. I awoke Saturday morning with every joint stiff. I could hardly move. I knew I'd spend the weekend in the nest, because my hosts didn't work weekends. When I heard them say they were going to the store, I sneaked out long enough to sit a while in the bathroom doing you know what. I took a coke, I popped some corn, I sprayed air freshener, and returned to my nest. Weekends were such joy!

I no longer felt that I was a thief since I raked the yard. It was a good thing I did too, because it began to rain late Saturday afternoon and continued on into Monday. I began to think about solving my pay back issue for October. I found myself talking to God. I don't know that I am religious. I've never been to church. But I do believe there is a God because someone is watching out for me. Anyway, I needed to talk to someone. It had been over a month since I had had a conversation. I explained all this to God and you know, I do believe the Spirit listened. I didn't have to wait long for an answer.

It was Monday morning. I was playing on the computer. Suddenly, the room got very dark. I realized the rain had developed into some type of major storm. I shut down the computer and turned on the TV. There were severe storm warnings and high wind warnings for just about everywhere. I turned off the TV and opened the back door a little. There was humid air that hung heavy on the trees. Nothing moved. It was totally silent outside. I quickly shut the door and turned to go to my nest, when the entire right side of the house lit up with a crack of lightening and a roll of thunder that made every window shake. I was stunned. It took me a moment to realize that the corner of the house was on fire. Big raindrops began to fall, and the wind whipped up into a frenzy.

I couldn't move for a few moments. I could see the bright orange fire; I could smell a strange smell. The hair on my arms stood up. When at last I could move, I grabbed the phone and dialed 911. "I live at 60 Mound Street in Milford, Ohio. The house is on fire. Come quick!" I shouted into the phone. The 911 operator wanted to asked me a lot of questions, but I just hung up. The house was getting smoky. I had to get out. I could hear sirens in the distance. I knew the firemen would go over this house with a fine-tooth comb. I couldn't leave the dog. I just couldn't. She was shaking too. I grabbed her up and ran out the back door into the alley.

I pretended to walk the dog so that I could watch the firemen. The storm had subsided to a drippy, wet rain. I heard the fireman say that the fire was mostly in the tree and the corner of the house. Because they got there so quickly, there really wasn't much damage to the house. There was a need for a little paint, and of course smoke clean up. I heard him say Mr. Gatch was on his way home, because he worked close by. That really panicked me. I didn't realize how close he was at all times. I saw Bill come home and open the front and back doors to let the smoke blow out. That is when he saw me in the alley.

"I guess you found our dog. She must have run out when the firemen came," he said.

"Yea, I didn't want her to get lost." I replied.

"Thanks for hanging on to her. I'd like to reward you." He reached in his pocket for a five-dollar bill.

"That's alright," I said, "All I did was pick her up. She seemed scared and shaky."

"Well thanks again." Bill took the dog and returned to the house.

I was on the outside looking in. I squished when I walked. I was soaking wet from head to foot. How was I going to get back inside without being seen? I walked around the block. Then I did it again trying to warm up. I saw Bill in the front yard trying to move the limbs that had fallen. It was now or never. I went to the back alley, worked my way up to the open back door, and in a flash, I was down in my nest. I left a trail of water wherever I walked. I pulled off my clothes and put them in a plastic bucket. I grabbed a rag and wiped up my footprints and hoped I would not have to crawl out naked.

I felt that saving the house and the dog paid for October. It was clear I needed an emergency plan in case something like this happened again. I made a list:

1. Find a change of clothes
2. Find some kind of coat
3. More food for weekends and sick days
4. Something to kill time like a hobby

That was all I remember because I fell asleep. When I awoke, Bill was retelling the story to Judy at dinner. "We were lucky. Because it was called in so fast, there was only smoke damage." Bill said. "I still can't figure out who it was that called it in."

Judy said, "We may never know. It could have been someone in a passing car even."

"There was a young boy who found Penny. I guess he could

have done it."

"Did you know him?"

"No, not really. But I had the feeling I should know him. Isn't that strange?"

Chapter 4

All Work And No Play Means You Got To Eat Candy

The last week of October rolled around with no other major problems. It was about one in the afternoon. I was playing on the computer when I heard a car door slam and someone talking. The voice sounded female. I switched off the computer and booked it to the nest. My heart had not slowed down when a lady and a little boy came into the basement. This had to be one of the daughters. She began to put in laundry, all the while chattering to the little boy. She pulled out a box of blocks, little animals, and school bus people for him to be entertained. He seemed happy with the plan. Suddenly the phone rang upstairs and she ran to answer it. Penny came sniffing around the toys. Penny, of course, knew about my nest. She decided to crawl back with me for a quick nap.

Watching Penny, Daniel decided to follow. I knew I was done for. Daniel came slowly back until he spied me. I thought he would yell or run to tell. He just got a big smile on his face and handed me a small cow. I smiled back. What else could I do? He jabbered a bunch of stuff and I didn't understand a word. I patted my chest and said softly, "Friend."

"Daniel, where did you go?" the lady called. "What are you doing under there? Come on out here."

Daniel crawled out and pointed to me and said, "Friend." The little snitch told on me. "You got a friend under there?" With that Penny came out. Boy, was I lucky. She thought Daniel was talking about the dog. "Come on now. I'll make lunch while the clothes wash."

For the moment, I was fine. I guess she put Daniel down for a nap, because he was gone while she finished her laundry. When Judy and Bill came home, the laundry was done and something was cooking that smelled wonderful. I could hear Daniel greet his grandparents and there was laughing. I found out he was just two years old. He wanted to come back to the basement, and finally, they came down with him. They laughed when he crawled into the nest. He jabbered away to me, and I made faces for him. He would laugh and laugh. They referred to me as Daniel's pretend friend. See, I told you I was invisible. They called him to leave for home, and that's when I heard something interesting. Sunday night was trick or treat night. The lady and Daniel would come about five to go begging at six. It seemed in this neighborhood you begged from six to eight. With that they left, and the house settled down for the night.

Candy! It had been such a long time since I had candy. If I could go trick or treating, I could get a bag of it for free. I would have to dress up and somehow get out of the house, but WOW! I'd be taking an awful chance. I thought about it all night. Was it possible?

The next day, I made a list of what I would have to do:

1. Get a costume.

2. Get out of the house.

That was about it, really. All I could think about was candy. I searched the house for a costume. I found a big brown sack that was all torn around one end. There was an old piece of rope, a torn red rag, and markers. You can do a lot with markers. I cut a whole for my head and arms in the bag. I stuffed a towel inside my shirt to make it look like a hump. I tied the red rag over one eye, like a pirate. I'd use the markers to put lines and black spots on my face. It just might work.

Sunday would be a tough day to get out of the house. If it was a pretty day, I could go out in the morning, when Judy goes to church and Bill gets coffee somewhere. That made the most sense. If it rained, well, I'd just have to hope it wouldn't. Luck was with me. Sunday came and it was sunny and about seventy degrees. With my packed lunch, I got out free and clear of the house. I walked up the alley and down by the Little Miami River. I laid on a warm rock and let the sun bake into my bones. It felt wonderful. Then I ate my apple and peanut butter sandwich and thought about my good fortune. In the late afternoon, I came back to Mound Street. Every house had boys and girls dressed up in costumes, jumping up and down on the porch. I didn't quite understand why they were waiting. A church bell began to ring, a siren began to blow, and all the kids ran off the porches. So this is how it is done in Milford. I was close to 60 Mound Street, and little Daniel ran up to me and grabbed my hand. "Friend," he said.

"I'm sorry," his mother said, "He thinks you are his imaginary friend."

"That's okay," I said. "He can walk with me." All of a sudden I had tears in my eyes. I felt like I was part of a real family. I took good care of him on the steps of the houses. The first house gave us Tootsies. The second gave us gum. The third gave us Snickers. I was having a great time. I held Daniel's hand and we walked together for about a block and a half. All the while he chattered away. At this point, he got tired and his mother said they would go home. She thanked me for being kind to Daniel and left. Now I could really move. I did Cleveland Avenue, Laurel Street, and went on to Gatch Street. A police car came by real slow. My heart beat so fast. I was afraid to glance their way. The other kids waved and yelled to the cops. They all ran to the cruiser. Can you believe it? The policemen gave out apples to all the trick or treaters. The officer said to listen for the siren and go home as soon as it blew. Everyone said they would. I couldn't believe this town.

Soon after that the siren did blow. The kids scattered and I headed home. That is when I discovered I had made a major mistake. I thought I had planned everything. What I forgot to plan was major. HOW WAS I GOING TO GET BACK INSIDE THE HOUSE? How could I be so stupid? I let candy rule my life. I had to think fast. There were these evergreen bushes in front of the house. I crawled behind them and ate candy. Sooner or later someone would come outside and maybe I could get in. I was very careful to keep all the wrappers in the bag, so I wouldn't leave a trail. My wonderful, lucky day was turning into a night of terror as it began to rain. The temperature dropped. The rain began to freeze. I hadn't thought about a coat when I left Sunday morning. I guess I slept a little, because when I came to myself, my stomach began to hurt. There was no traffic and no people. I was really in a fix. I'll admit I prayed a little. Do you think God will help you when you are greedy for candy and stupid?

It didn't take too much longer for my prayer to be answered.

Penny began to bark, and bark, and bark. They tried to let her out in the backyard, but she still carried on. I heard Bill say that she would wake the neighbors, so he put her on a leash and came out the front door with her and walked up the block. Quick as a flash I was at that front door hoping it wasn't locked. I turned the knob, the door opened, and I was inside. I nearly doubled over with stomach pains. I knew I'd never make it to the basement nest. I headed for the nest in the computer room. Safely hidden, I shivered, and shivered, and shivered. The pains grew worse. I was about to throw up. Throwing caution to the wind, I wiggled out from under the bed and hit the bathroom on the run. I threw up, I pooped, I threw up again, and then I pooped again. At last feeling like a rag doll, I went back under the bed. Now the bathroom is next to the bedroom where Judy and Bill sleep. I knew I woke Judy up. Penny was still keeping Bill busy. She didn't get up to see what was going on.

"Are you alright?" Judy called, when I came out.

"Yea," I replied in a deeper voice.

A few minutes later, Bill and Penny came back inside. I had glanced at the clock in the bathroom and knew it was about four in the morning. I must have drifted off or fainted or something, because the next thing I knew, they were up for work.

"You were really sick last night," Judy said. "Are you feeling better now?"

"I wasn't sick," Bill replied. "What gave you that idea?"

"I heard you throwing up in the middle of the night."

"Not me, I was out with Penny. She had a barking fit. I never did figure out what her problem was. You must have been dreaming."

"It couldn't have been a dream. It was so real. I asked if you were okay and you said, 'Yea'."

"See, you were dreaming. When do I ever say 'yea'?" With that they left for work.

I could hardly move. I got to the bathroom and ran a hot bath. I was so weak. I knew I had a fever. I forced myself to wash quickly, because I was still chilling. It was hard getting the marker off. I found a thermometer and took my temperature. It said 102 degrees. My mom had taught me to read a thermometer when my sister was born. I knew this couldn't be good. I also knew that I was not sick from eating candy. This had to be some kind of bug. I didn't want food. I would just throw it up anyway. I found some aspirin and took two. I took six more with me for later. I stole two Cokes, got a plastic bucket to throw up in, if it came to that, and my Clorox bottle full of water. With all this, I made my way to the basement. I crawled into that sleeping bag and didn't move.

I woke up when they came home from work, but didn't move. My head was pounding. I heard something about Penny finding a bag of candy that they thought was Daniel's. I didn't even care. I went back to sleep until ten the next morning. I was able to get to the bathroom and make a cup of tea. I ate one piece of toast. I took two boxes of lemon Jello to mix with water to drink, like my mother always did when we were sick, and I took another Coke. I'm sure they'll miss the Coke, but I just didn't care. I went back to the nest for two more days.

Chapter 5

Worries and Memories

I was slowly getting well, even though I was still very weak. I laid around most of the time. I worried about how I could repay my hosts for the extra Coke and other stuff I had used during my illness. Judy had come home from work one day and announced that the house smelled like a sick house. My heart nearly crawled out of my mouth. I thought for sure I would be found. Instead, on the weekend, she began cleaning top to bottom. The curtains came down and were washed. Windows and walls were cleaned. The floors were polished with good smelling wax. During all this, I drifted in and out of sleep. I had bad dreams of things I hadn't thought about in years.

I remembered that when I was in the first grade there was a boy in my class named Lenny. He only talked using one or two words. He would say "Hi," "No," and if he didn't understand or know the answer, he'd say "Stupid head!" First graders didn't really understand the meaning of words, but we did understand that it meant that Lenny didn't understand what was happening. I believe that the teacher understood that too, but she pretended she didn't. Every time Lenny said it, she would smack him. Then of course, he would say it again. Then she would hit him again. Once the principal came in and pulled Lenny out of the room by his foot. I was in the hall at the time because it was my turn to use the bathroom. He yanked him down the steps, hitting his head on each step. Lenny just kept yelling, "Stupid head!"

The principal saw me and yelled, "Get Where You Belong!" I never said a word about what I saw and neither did my teacher. I felt so bad for Lenny because hitting wasn't allowed in our state. I would always be nice to him after that. I'd give him my lunch snack. He'd just smile at me. One day he just disappeared. The kids said they sent him to stupid school. I never was sure where he went; he just disappeared. I didn't understand at the time that Lenny was special. I thought the teachers always did the right thing. Now, I feel so sick and sad, I don't want to move. Why did grownups treat Lenny like that?

Slowly I drifted back to sleep. At least I think it was sleep. It all seemed so real. I was in the fourth grade. There were two boys in my class named Mason and Martin. They came as new boys. They had red hair and wore glasses. They were good boys and followed all the rules. They were not good students and always got a F on their papers. Every time the teacher would call on them, the teacher would roll his eyes and tell them that they were stupid. If they told about a trip or event they had experienced, the teacher would call them liars. Sometimes the rest of us would speak up and say they were telling the truth. But the teacher didn't stop making fun of them. Why did I dream of these bad people? Why didn't I dream about the four nice teachers I had in fifth grade? They made me feel so special each and every day. One would stay after each day and help me with math. I stayed every day just to be treated kindly. The others would let us get extra water on hot days and help me write stories. I loved that. Why can't all teachers be like that?

Lilly was the nicest girl in class. She was really kind and nice to everybody, even me. When she would bring candy in her lunch, she would share with all of us, even if it meant that she only got one piece. Every teacher and every student liked her. A teacher from another class was supposed to get kids to write stories for the school paper. She was to get one kid from each class. She came in when our teacher was out and the substitute told her to come back when the teacher returned. She just asked, "Who is the best kid in the class?" The sub told her it was Lilly. The teacher wrote it on a list.

Lilly wasn't there that day, so she knew nothing about it. The teacher forgot to tell Lilly or the regular teacher the next day so no one knew anything about it. The principal asked the teacher about the stories but she forgot to collect any stories from any of the classes. The principal was really upset. He was yelling at her in the hall. Our door was open and I sat by it, so I could hear everything. That teacher said it wasn't her fault, it was Lilly's. The teacher said Lilly was rude and refused to complete the assignment, and that Lilly told other kids not to do it either. The principal called Lilly out into the hall and asked her why she didn't write the story. Lilly said she didn't know what they were talking about. The principal thought she wasn't telling the truth, so he made her stay in every day for a week during lunch. Lilly's mom came in to talk to the teacher, but the teacher started yelling and crying and said everyone was against her. The Mom couldn't do anything but walk away. Man, I wish I could get my way just by crying and yelling. But Lilly kept on smiling. She said she'd stay in for a week, she didn't care. She said she would just pray for that crazy teacher.

We got even though. The entire class collected candy or gum and gave some to Lilly every day she had to stay in. We took turns not turning in our homework, so there would always be someone inside with her. Why would a teacher do that to a really good kid? I never thought a teacher would lie like that. I had almost forgotten this story. I don't know why I remembered it except I had so much time on my hands.

I came to myself thinking about Mr. E. who slipped me two dollars so I could go on the class picnic. He let me wear his tie so I could go to the concert. Why can't I dream about him? I wouldn't wake up trembling inside.

There were two men who worked with the big kids. If you used the bathroom in their hall, or complained because their students roughed you up at lunch, they'd snatch you up and drag you in the storage room where no one could see, and poke you really hard in the chest with their finger. It hurt so bad you couldn't get your breath. It hurt too bad to even cry. They shook you like you were a sound sleeper. We all knew they did it. They did it to me once because they thought I was someone else. When they realized their mistake, they gave me candy and said a big man never tells on people. No one ever told on them. There is no use. Who would believe it? I know the principal knows because one kid tried to tell him. He just said, "You probably deserved it." Why do great big people like to beat up on smaller ones?

I shook myself awake and tried to calm myself with a good thought. The school wouldn't let us celebrate Christmas. So this one teacher let us decorate butcher paper with anything we wanted. She said the next day there would be a test. Anyone who got an A would get a prize. The next day the test had ten questions like, "What is your name? What is your favorite color? What did you have for lunch?" We thought she was crazy. Of course everyone got an A. We all got a motorized car wrapped in our very own paper. She reminded us that they were not Christmas presents. I loved her. If I ran a school, all the teachers would be like her.

I drifted back to sleep thinking about the old lady down the street who was going blind. She wouldn't allow anyone to pity her. She said she would make use of the eyesight she had left. She knitted sweaters for everyone in the class. They were the kind that you pull over your head. There was all colors. We got to pick out the one we liked best. I heard somebody tell my teacher that she should keep them and sell them for a pretty penny. I think that means lots of money. My teacher said it was rude to sell a gift. My little sister is still wearing my sweater.

When we went to Science, the teacher was a sub who would be there until the end of the year. He always showed a film. He called Paula to come stand by him. Paula is really cute but really slow. The teacher would put his hand under her skirt. Paula just giggled and would say, "No, No!" We told her not to do it but he said he would put her in detention if she disobeyed him. She was scared of him and scared of how mad her mom would be if she got detention. Why would a grownup man need to play in a little girl's underpants? None of us told. I don't know why little kids are like that. The next year he got arrested at another school.

Last year's teacher said we could all go to the circus if we brought in two dollars. We all did, but it wasn't easy. Nothing went wrong; nobody did anything that we remembered. The day of the trip, the teacher said we couldn't go, because we were bad. He said schools don't give refunds. That wasn't the only time that happened either. Two other events were canceled. That was fifty dollars from our class alone. I washed my neighbor's car for nothing. Why do teachers have to steal money from kids and why does the school let them? All of these stories kept going through my mind as I drifted in and out of sleep.

I woke up today feeling better and I promised myself that from now on I would only remember pleasant things. One really great day was the day my teacher had a birthday party for Dr. Martin Luther King. We had cake with roses on it, and hats. We each got a book about Dr. King. She said if Dr. King had his way, no one would get his birthday off. We would add a week to the school year because he valued education. Also, we would spend his birthday helping others. We had a great day. I have always tried to find someone to help on Dr. King's Birthday.

I won't tell anyone about this. When my Daddy went to jail, one teacher got us a heater and came and hooked it up. Another lady, who had flu, got us food and money so welfare wouldn't take us away from Mom. Another lady took my sister and me shopping for new clothes and coats and hats. We got just what we wanted. We didn't have to wear the coats foster kids get. You know the ones that are all alike. They even got my little sister a stuffed bear to hug. They all told us not to tell. They said, "Food feeds the body, but toys feed the soul."

Remembering the good things made me feel great. I also realized I can't hide here forever. I don't know just what to do about that. I'll think on it. I know I can exist the four days during Thanksgiving, but I'm worried about the two weeks during Christmas. I needed to make plans.

Chapter 6

Clayborn Jackie

The bad flu was now in the past and Thanksgiving is this Thursday. Dinnertime talk became very interesting tonight. It seems that Bill and Judy are leaving Thursday morning to have Thanksgiving with Judy's sister who lives in Springfield. The nice part is that they are staying the weekend. They won't come home until Sunday afternoon. I'll have almost four days with no pressure or fear. I had the feeling that this was like a school holiday.

Sure enough, Bill and Judy left the house by nine in the

morning. I had a long bath and ate a big breakfast. They had left the dog with a friend. I really missed the dog. Around noon it began to snow. It was a snow that fell fast and deep and hard. I couldn't resist going out to play in it. I met the boys that I had played basketball with the first day I came to Milford and we threw snowballs for a while. I realized that I looked really ragged compared to them. I came at the beginning of the school year with only a T-shirt and shorts. I had no winter coat or any other winter clothes. I had found a pair of Judy's old pants when I was looking for my Halloween costume. I had grown a lot since then and my pants were too short. My shoes were too small. My hair had grown back in, but I really needed a haircut. About six o'clock that night the snow stopped. There were at least a good two feet. The boys went in for dinner and so did I. I got something to eat and turned on the TV. It said they didn't expect any more snow. I grabbed my snow shovel and started on the front walk. My muscles felt good having something to do. I figured this would pay for all the food and medicine I took during the flu. I was feeling good. I was getting ready to go inside when a man from the apartment building walked over and asked me to clean his walks on Friday. He said he would pay me. I agreed and went inside a happy man.

The next day I was up and shoveling early. A lady stopped her car and said she lived up the street and needed her walk shoveled. I agreed. While I was shoveling that walk, another neighbor asked me to clean her walk. By two o'clock on Friday I had close to seventy dollars. I couldn't believe it. In the course of the day and talking to people, I learned that there were fast food restaurants and a thrift store a mile away. Saturday I planned on going on an adventure.

I was up and dressed in my ratty clothes early. I had had breakfast and was headed out the door. I passed that barbershop I had seen the day I arrived. This was the kind where men go, not girls. I decided it was time for a MAN haircut. I went in and took a seat. I noticed that after the men had their hair cut, they gave extra money to the barber. I guess that was a tip. I wouldn't have thought to tip. The barber called me up and asked me who had cut my hair last. I told him my head was shaved, that I had had no hair. He looked sad and gave me a great haircut. I never looked so good. He only charged me six bucks. I gave him a buck tip. I don't know why he was sad. I think he thought I was sick. I walked across the street to the thrift store. I got a real nice zip up coat with a hood for four dollars. I got two pairs of jeans for three dollars each. I found a pack of underwear and a pack of socks. They were two bucks a pack. I got two sweatshirts and two T-shirts for another ten dollars. I still had a ton of money left. I decided to go out for lunch. I planned to eat at Frisch's now and take Skyline home for dinner. Lunch was great. I had a Big Boy with fries and coleslaw. I had pumpkin pie since it was Thanksgiving weekend. Then I headed for Skyline.

I got my to go order and went out the door. I couldn't believe what I saw. Clayborn Jackie was getting out of a big white truck. He didn't see me, thank goodness. Now Clayborn Jackie is bad news. He is about sixteen and packs heat. He hurts people, he steals, he lies, he has been arrested fifty times, and he is still on the street. I knew when he got out of that truck, he was up to no good. He went in Skyline and sat down. I watched for a few minutes, then I checked out the truck. I memorized the plate number. I slowly pulled open the back of the truck. The truck was full of televisions, computers, and stuff like that. I closed up the truck and got out of there quick. I didn't need him seeing me. I was shaking when I got home. I couldn't get Clayborn out of my head. I knew he was a crook. I also knew he would hurt me bad if he found me. He didn't need a reason. Not only would he hurt me, but Mom and my little sister too. The late news reported a lot of break-ins in this area. They asked people to be on the lookout. I may be only guessing, but I knew Clayborn and his friends were the ones doing it. I didn't think that I could do anything about it. If I tried, I would be found out and I would have to leave.

I tossed and turned all night. It had dawned on me when I had flu, that I couldn't stay here forever. I was going to have to leave. I didn't want to go. I longed to stay here. I guess I wanted to be Bill and Judy's kid. I wanted to live upstairs and eat at their table. I wanted them to fuss over me like they did Daniel. In my heart I knew this could never be. But I felt sad when I thought about leaving.

Sunday they returned and so did the dog. Gosh I missed that dog. I had to stay hidden all day. I heard Bill ask, "Who shoveled the walk?" Judy pointed out that over the past year many nice things had happened to them that they couldn't explain. I could tell they liked it but were getting curious. "I think I'll ask the neighbors to keep an eye out. Maybe we can find out who our good fairy is," Bill said.

I DID NOT like being a fairy, that's for sure. I realized I was going to have to leave. I may have to do it in a hurry one day. I had a little money left. It would be enough for a bus ticket and some food. I made a plan. I put my money and extra clothes in a bag. Every night when I was done writing, I put that in the bag too. I planned to sit tight and try to make it through the winter, but I was ready if and when I had to leave.

Chapter 7

Christmas

Christmas was just around the corner. I was a nervous wreck. I couldn't store enough food for two weeks in my nest. They would be home. There would be all kinds of company. They kept talking about Ann coming in for the holidays. They worried about her flight being on time if it snowed. She didn't eat meat, so they worried about what to cook for her. She is the other daughter. I don't think she has kids. What was I going to do? This book I had found on the shelf with the family Bible, said that all you had to do was pray and God would answer your prayers. I didn't believe in fairy tales anymore, but

I did do some powerful praying even though I didn't expect things to change. I pushed the problem to the back of my mind. It sat there like a stone. I guess I am still a stupid kid, because all I could think about was Christmas.

I really wanted to give Bill and Judy a gift. I couldn't think of anything they wanted that I could afford. Also, I wanted my little sister to have something. I didn't know how I could manage that. I knew the school would give my sister one of those see through stockings with candy and a card board game where you put the bead in the holes. It was nice to get something, but that really wasn't Santa Claus. The first part of my giving problem was solved when I heard Judy worrying over getting the house clean for Christmas, and when would she have time to make cookies? She was so worried that she seemed to be making herself sick. I could clean the house okay, but the cookies would be a challenge. The cleaning would need to be done just before the holiday. She said she would be working until the day before Christmas Eve. She worried about something called the filthy rag on the front door. I figured out she meant the curtain. I needed a plan.

The next day I read cookbooks. Sugar cookies were easy and looked like fun. There was something called Russian tea cakes that looked good. There were lemon bars that I would love. These cookies could be done in advance and hidden until needed. Here was my plan:

1. Wash the filthy rag.
2. Bake sugar cookies early and air out the house so they don't smell.
3. Bake Russian tea cakes and do the airing thing.
4. Make lemon bars and air the house.
5. Scrub the bathroom walls, floor, and all.
6. Clean the house.

I checked to see if all the supplies were on hand. I was really looking forward to doing this, and my problems seemed far, far away.

Two weeks before Christmas a snowstorm hit. It was an unusual storm. There was ice underneath and a foot of snow on top. To make things worse, it was cold outside, really cold. I got my shovel the next morning and got started. It was slow going, because the ice didn't want to go. I got the snow off and salted the ice, and waited for the sun. The apartment man asked me again to do his walk, and so did the lady down the street. They wanted their cars cleaned off too. It was really hard work. Half way through, I hurt everywhere and wanted to quit. I just kept picturing dollar signs. I got the job done and the cash was in my hand. I was getting ready to leave when the lady stopped me.

"I need a dog sitter for the week of Christmas break. Are you interested? It pays ten dollars a day. I'll give you a key to the house and you can let the dog out twice a day, and maybe play with him a little. What do you think?"

I didn't hear anything after "TEN DOLLARS A DAY."

"Sure, I'll do that," I finally said.

"Now give me your name and phone number."

I was in shock. I didn't know what to do. I couldn't give her my real name. I stammered out, "Jacob Adams, but I don't have a phone."

"Where do you live Jacob?" she asked. "I stay with my grandma down the street sometimes." I replied.

"Well, you stop in tomorrow and I'll give you a key and you can meet the dog."

I hurried home because it was getting late in the day. I told her I would see her the next day. I wanted to soak in the tub. I ached all over, but there just wasn't time. I was safely in my nest when what I had agreed to do finally hit me. I'd get a key to a house. I would make a lot of money. Maybe I could stay there during the holiday. Maybe God did hear me. I felt something deep inside, like somebody somewhere did love me. Am I feeling God? If so, why didn't I feel him before? The only thing I could figure was that my life was now peaceful. I had time to think. I had time to wonder. I had time to feel. I liked it. I had time for God. Maybe, God had time for me too.

I returned to the lady's house the next day. I learned how the locks worked. The dog was called Rippy. He was a very friendly black and white little hound dog. We got along immediately. She said her plane would leave at 8:00 A.M. on the twenty-fourth. She would return the day after New Years. I took the key and we agreed that she would call me at her house at six every evening, when I was there to feed the dog. My mind was going so fast. I was excited. I would be safe during the holidays. I'd need food. I couldn't take two weeks worth from Bill and Judy. I couldn't eat the lady's food. She would notice. I'd need to shop. Out came the cookbooks. I made notes. I could cook a chicken, sweet potatoes, Jello. In other words, I could make my own holiday dinner. I would take my crackers and peanut butter. I got a bigger bag to pack.

The next day my work began. I washed the filthy rag and hung it back on the door. I made the sugar cookies. Mrs. Bea had had me read her the directions once when she was making cookies. She taught me all the short spellings like tsp for teaspoon. I used cookie cutters for the first time ever. I had Christmas trees, dogs, bells, bows, Santa Claus, a gingerbread man, a snowman and an angel. It was so much fun. I had never done any of this in my life. By noon the curtain was up, the cookies were done and the mess was cleaned up. The windows were opened and the house was aired out. I sprayed air freshener. I found a couple of containers with lids in the basement. One was big and the other was little. I washed them and lined them with foil like Mrs. Bea had shown me. I stored the cookies in them. I filled up the big tin and had ten cookies left. I put them in the smaller tin. I only put in six. I ate four of them. They were wonderful. I was safely back in my nest and no one seemed to notice. The next day I did tea cakes and lemon bars with the same results. Once again I searched for containers. I didn't have any luck, so I wrapped them in foil. You can learn a lot reading cookbooks. Tomorrow the cleaning would begin big time.

This housewife work is for the birds. Scrubbing down the bathroom was not fun. I was afraid of getting bleach on my clothes, so I did the work without any clothes. My mom always made me use bleach in the bathroom and kitchen to kill germs and mold. It didn't take that long. It was just that I hated it and it hurt my arms. By noon I was finished. I decided to take a walk. Up by the mall was a Dollar Store and an Odd Lots. I didn't plan to Christmas shop, it just happened. I found a dress-up doll and some clothes for it. My sister would love that. There was a cute, stuffed, floppy-eared dog that was cheap. I found a nice sweater at the thrift store for my mom. I had no idea how I could give them these things. I just ached to do it though. I wanted so much for them to be happy and as peaceful as I was. I had chili for lunch. I loved having a little money on me.

The next day I finished cleaning the house. I didn't air out the house. I wanted Judy to know that the work had been done. I even did the laundry and had it folded and on hangers. Judy was surprised. She thought her daughter did it. She told everyone about her wonderful daughter on the phone that night. I also heard her say that her daughter Ann was coming for Christmas. She sounded so excited. I didn't realize grownups enjoyed Christmas that much. She said Ann would sing at a coffeehouse while she was here. Judy was really looking forward to the entire family going to see the show. I wished I could see her perform and be part of the family. I won't even get to see her, because I'll be hiding up the street.

The next day was December the twenty-third, Judy's last day of work. I had to get out of the house by four o'clock. It was forecasted to be clear but cold. It would be in the twenties. When I woke up, I put on all my clothes, one layer on top of another. I rolled my sleeping bag up and put it in a plastic bag. I had my bag of gifts and the small container of cookies. I took an old coffee can, not the plastic one. I filled it with charcoal and put matches in my pocket. That was the only thing my dad ever taught me. We'd grill on a coffee can. I packed hot chocolate mix, two peanut butter and jelly sandwiches, an apple, and a Clorox bottle of clean water. I waited and waited. At four o'clock I put the cookies I had baked on the kitchen table and left by the back door. I headed for the river. There had to be a place to hide somewhere. No one paid any attention to me. I saw only a car or two go by. I was still invisible.

I found a rocky area that looked like someone had dumped big rocks there, maybe to keep the hill from sliding. I stacked the rocks I could lift to make a sort of wind block on three sides. This hid me from the river and from the opposite shore. I could still be seen from the sky. I didn't like that much and I'm not sure why. I gathered some brush and put it in on top for a cover. As an after - thought, I put some heavier rocks on top of the brush. It was nearly dark. I checked again to make sure I had the house keys, food supplies, and money. I got in the sleeping bag and pulled it up to my ears. I have to say my thrift store coat was really warm. I didn't want to light the charcoal until I absolutely had to do it. The cold was slowly creeping into my body. I thought to myself that I should be very unhappy, but the sky was so beautiful. The stars were outstanding. I was spellbound by the stars. I wasn't unhappy. I was rather pleased with myself.

Chapter 8

Terrified

I guess the cold got to me, because even though it was early, I fell asleep. It was a good sleep. I felt like I had slept a long time. I awoke suddenly and felt like something was wrong. I laid very still and let my eyes become accustomed to the dark. I didn't move a muscle. I turned my head ever so slightly. That is when I noticed four yellow eyes looking at me. Slowly I reached for my can of charcoal and lit the coals. Until the coals got started, there was a short orange flame. I now could see my visitors' faces. Although they looked like dogs, I realized they had long pointy ears. Their coats were yellowish brown. They were very skinny, obviously not someone's pets. In the distance, I heard a coyote howl. Not that I had ever heard a coyote howl, but it did sound just like the movies. I'm a city boy. What do I know about coyotes? I knew that they have packs. I knew that they could be dangerous. I knew I was in trouble.

I boiled water for hot chocolate. I refilled the small pot and boiled more. I was guessing I could always throw it at the coyotes, if push came to shove. I was less frightened after the hot chocolate, until I felt something jump on my makeshift roof. I knew in an instant that that was more of the pack. I realized I had to stay put. At least three sides and my head were protected. I sipped hot chocolate and waited, and waited, and waited. Time passed so slowly. The good thing was that I forgot to be cold. It appeared the darkness was beginning to lighten up ever so slightly. I took out my sandwiches and tore them in half. I tossed half to my two visitors. The coyotes swallowed in a flash. These were my enemies, but I felt sorry for them. I felt the one on the roof jump down, and the rest followed him off in the distance. I counted five in all. This was a great story, but who would believe it? At least I know I am not invisible. The coyotes saw me.

I pulled myself together and put out my coals. I bagged up my sleeping bag. I don't know what time the sun comes up in the winter, but I'm guessing about seven thirty. If the lady was leaving on a plane at eight, then she would leave for the airport by six. I was guessing it was okay for me to go to the house. When I got to Mound Street, I saw her pull out of the driveway. I waited to see if she was coming back. I thought maybe she went after coffee. When she didn't return, I went in. I was glad to be warm, and the dog nearly licked me to death. I didn't turn on any lights. I made a cup of tea and ate a piece of toast. I turned on cartoons. It had been a long time since I watched those. The plan for the day began to come together in my head:

1. I'd walk the dog.

2. I'd walk down to the bus and ride to the city.

3. I'd drop off my Christmas gifts to my sister and mom (hopefully without being seen).

4. Catch the bus back and go to the store.

5. Be home by six when the lady is going to call.

It sounded simple enough. The dog walking and bus catching sounded simple. It had been a long time since I had been to Fountain Square. It would be nice all done up for the holidays. It was a long walk to my side of town, but I made it without being seen. It wasn't ten o'clock yet. I knew Mom would be at work. With luck Dad would be gone. Slowly I made my way up the stairs and turned the knob. It was locked. That was new. They never locked the door. I felt around for a key but found none. I could hear the cartoons inside. My sister was there, hopefully alone. I tapped gently on the door. Her eyes peered out at me in great surprise. I quickly told her not to scream. I asked where Dad was and she said he hadn't come home from the night before yet. I hugged her and she hugged me. She still had her long hair. I was so glad. I told her she must tell no one that I came. I gave her the gift and told her to give Mom hers on Christmas. She wanted to know where I had been, but all I would say was somewhere safe. I handed her the cookies and told her to hide them in a safe place. I said, "I made these just for you and you are the only one that can eat them." She said Dad was meaner than ever and that she tried to just stay out of his way.

That is when we heard the familiar stomp on the stairs. She

began to shake. I told her to hide and I'd take care of it. I hid behind the skinny Christmas tree my mom had managed to get. Dad was drunk, he was loud, and he was really mad, and there was no one to argue with him. He kicked off his shoes and threw them as hard as he could knocking over a lamp. All the old fears were back in my gut. I could never come back to this. I knew that now. For no reason, he attacked the Christmas Tree. He knocked it over and began to stomp on it. He broke it in half. That is when he realized I was standing there. He didn't recognize me at first. He reached to grab me, but I just put out my hand and stared at him. He stammered, "Are you a ghost? You look like my dead son."

"I am your dead son, you fool!" I said. "You will pay for your actions!" With that he began to cry. He staggered to his bed and passed out. I knew he would not remember any of this. I helped my sister clean up the mess. The tree was broken in half, but the top part was okay. I put the top back in the stand and set it up on an end table. We took a sheet and covered the end table. It looked like a tree on a mountain. I took my sister's hand and we walked up to the Dollar Store. I bought two boxes of ornaments and a box of candy canes. On the way home, we stopped for a hamburger and fries. My sister looked at me as if I was some kind of hero. This would cut down on my grocery money, but it was worth it. I could eat peanut butter forever.

When we got home, I helped her decorate the tree. It looked really nice. I told her to tell Mom that the church lady brought the stuff. I gave her the cookies I made and reminded her that they were just for her and to hide them in her bedroom. She cried when it was time for me to leave, but I had to go. I told her my life was in her hands and to try really hard not to tell that I was there. Then I opened the door and left her crying in the living room. It broke my heart. I couldn't stop the tears. I cried all the way back to Fountain Square. I cried on the bus. I cried most of the way back to Milford before I could stop.

I rode the bus to the end of the line, because it was closer to the store. I checked my money and walked inside. I got a roasting chicken and a box of dressing. I got bread. I got a small bag of baking potatoes. I didn't like vegetables much, so I got a bag that had two apples, two oranges, and two bananas. I got a liter of Coke and popcorn. I bought a cake, a pretty cake. It was marked down because of Christmas Eve. It looked so good and I didn't even know what kind it was. I had figured the cost and I was within pennies at the checkout. I had four bags to carry. They were heavier than I thought, but I knew I could do it. I started the long, cold walk home. It was about two miles, maybe a bit more. I had to walk as fast as I could, because the lady was going to call at six. It was already five thirty.

I walked in at five 'til six. The dog was glad to see me. I let him out in the yard and watched him do his business. He was glad to come back in. I fixed his dinner and gave him fresh water. With that, the phone rang. Yes, I had fed the dog; yes, I had let him out; yes, he had fresh water. That is when she asked me to bring in the mail. I said I would. Then she said the fifty dollars was behind a photo on the table in the living room. She thought I might want to spend it during the holidays. I really thanked her. That was it. My day was over. I put the leash on Rippy and walked him for fifteen minutes.

When I got home, I didn't turn on any lights. I was afraid the TV could be seen from the street by the neighbors. I walked through the house and found a small sitting room, upstairs, in the back of the house. It looked like a room for arts and crafts and stuff like that. It did have a small TV in it. I got a bag of popcorn, a banana, and some Coke, and made myself at home. Rippy loved sleeping by me in this little room.

Chapter 9

Lazy Days

I awoke Christmas Day still feeling sad because I had to leave my sister in that mess. Maybe he could have gotten help at one time, but I'm not sure he could now. Anyway, all those rehab places are for rich people. I can't see any AA sponsors driving to our part of town to talk someone out of a drink. Church groups come, but Dad would never go. I don't think he can help himself anymore. I don't understand Mom though. She loves us, I'm sure. She works hard. Why does she let him smack us around and use up all her money? I just don't get it. She is a good woman, yet I am madder at her than I am at him.

I felt better after I fed and walked Rippy. I dug out my notes on how to bake a chicken from the cookbook I had read. I let water run through it, because Mom did that. I found a roasting pan with a lid. I figured that would keep grease from making the oven dirty. I stuck in a potato to bake. I cooked the dressing on top of the stove. I chopped up an apple and mixed peanut butter with it. At two o'clock I had a feast. I sat down and ate and watched a Christmas movie.

I cleaned up really good. I took Rippy out to play a while. At five-forty-five, I fed him and gave him fresh water. At six, the lady called. At eight we had another walk. Then I went to sleep just like I belonged there. That is pretty much the way it went for the next week. On New Year's Eve, the lady called and said she would be home by noon on January second. I told her fine. I said I would walk the dog before school and check on everything. I did that, plus I dusted and cleaned the room I was in and the bathroom. I bagged up all my trash and put it in someone else's trashcan. I made sure I left no food or grocery bags that would look out of place. Since I had stolen a key for Bill and Judy's, I waited until I knew they were at work. Then I walked in like I owned the joint. I stored everything in my nest and I played with the dog. It was great to be home.

I fell into my old routine, but I had a nagging feeling that I needed to leave. Some pioneer I turned out to be. I was afraid to leave. Still I made sure I was always packed up. I threw myself into those school books Judy had for my grade. She even had test practice books. I did those like they were puzzles. I got pretty good. There were three more snows, and I saved every bit of money I earned.

February came with its cold, freezing days. I was almost at the point of forgetting about leaving. I was going out into the community almost three times a week. My body craved the exercise. I even got another haircut and bought more clothes at the thrift store. I looked good. I was content.

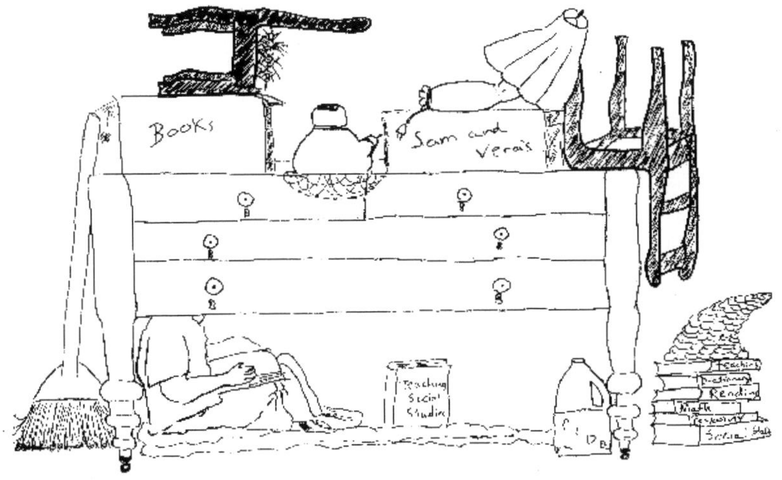

Chapter 10

Return of Clayborn Jackie

It was early, but Bill and Judy had left for work. I don't know why I was in the dining room looking out the front window, but I was. That is when I saw Clayborn Jackie's truck pull up to the house across the street. The minute I saw it, I remembered the plate number on the truck. I just couldn't let him hurt my world. I saw them go in and start putting stuff in the truck. What I did next, I did without thinking. I grabbed the phone. I told 911 what was going on. I told them the plate number. I told them his name and where he was from.

You know how 911 likes to keep you on the phone, but I couldn't do that. I hung up the phone and unlocked the front door. I ran out to the truck. I didn't hear the police, so I slid under the truck and started letting the air out of the tires. I had succeeded in flattening two tires when I looked up to see Clayborn standing there. He didn't recognize me all cleaned up. I saw the rage in his face. Grabbing my leg, he pulled me out from under the truck. He hit me upside the head so hard that the lights went off, then on, then off. He pounded me some more, but I was in no shape to feel it.

I came to myself in the back of his truck with blood everywhere. I pulled off my T-shirt and tried to mop up the blood. I could only see out of one eye. I could hear the police cars coming. I had to get out of there. Clayborn was trying to drive that truck with two flats, but he wasn't doing a very good job. Police cars were getting louder and louder. I was finding it hard to move or think. I tried the door, but it wouldn't budge. I prayed really hard for a way out of this. I didn't want the police to think I was part of this. I didn't want to lose my hiding place.

Suddenly, Clayborn lost control of the truck and it hit

something hard. With that the back door flew open and I rolled out on the ground. I could see the lights of the police cars on the far end of the street. I rolled under a parked car and laid still. The police pulled up the road by the truck. I saw them handcuff Clayborn and his two friends and put them in the car. Then one policeman yelled at the others. He was holding up my bloody shirt. Yellow crime tape came out and went around the truck. The car with Clayborn in it took off. The second car left one man to watch the truck and headed back down the street. I crawled out and limped back between two houses to the alley. Slowly I made my way home. Sure enough the police were at the house across the street. They were looking at my blood on the street. When they went in the house, I sneaked in through the front door.

My heart was still beating fast when I looked in the bathroom mirror. My left eye was already puffed up and shut. The entire side of my face was turning blue. There was a three inch gash on my head from hitting a jagged rock when I landed on the street. The cut had caused all the bleeding, and my left rib cage was bruised. I knew I was in bad shape and needed a doctor, but I couldn't go. I was afraid they would think I was working with Clayborn Jackie.

I quickly jumped into the shower and soaped off all the blood. My heart rate was beginning to slow, and I was cold, so cold my teeth were chattering. I didn't know what was going on, but I knew it wasn't good. I got a package of frozen mixed vegetables from the freezer to put on my eye and cut. I grabbed a coke and filled my container with water. As an afterthought, I swiped the aspirin. My head was spinning when I crawled into my nest. I was cold, so cold. I began to shake and I couldn't stop. I don't know if I fell asleep or fainted. All I know is that when I woke up, Bill and Judy were home and I hurt so bad.

I could hear their agitated voices and hear the TV. I wanted to listen, but within seconds, I drifted off again. The next thing I knew, they were leaving for work and it was morning. The pain was severe. I tried to get up. I managed to pull on clothes and crawl upstairs to the bathroom. My eye and face were as black as the tar on the road. I made a cup of tea and sipped it. It didn't stay down. I threw up instantly. I hurt too bad to cry. It was all I could do to get back in the nest. That is the way it went for the next week. I was dizzy when I was up. I threw up when I ate. And my head oozed sticky stuff in my hair and on my face. I longed for the news but always fell asleep. I heard bits and pieces from Bill and Judy:

1. There was a break in.

2. The good fairy had called it in to 911.

3. The police caught them, but found blood at the scene.

4. There was no body and nobody reported missing.

That was the limit of my information on what happened to Clayborn and his crew. That evening a policeman came to the house. They said the 911 call registered 60 Mound Street. Bill and Judy denied knowing anything about that. They told about the lightening strike that set the corner of the house on fire and how a call was made then. Of course they could prove they were at work. The police walked through the house. They even came downstairs and looked around. Just like that they left. They said that they were visiting everyone on the street. I went back to sleep.

It was a week or more before I could get up without being dizzy. I could eat toast and tea without throwing up. Bill and Judy's daughter was stopping by every day to check on the house. She came about one in the afternoon, when Daniel got out of nursery school.

Because of all the trouble on the street, Bill had hooked up a small TV in the basement, so he could watch the news while playing with his train. That made it easy on me. I could watch and then hide quickly, when the daughter showed up. At noon, I turned on the news. I was in shock. Clayborn Jackie was being held on a long list of charges - the worst being murder - MY MURDER! It seemed my mom gave my toothbrush to the police. The DNA matched my bloody shirt in the truck. He was going to jail this time. There was just one problem. I wasn't dead. The police thought Clayborn had kidnapped me back in the fall and then beat me to death. The two people with him were talking up a storm. They lived in fear of Clayborn, but didn't want murder charges. I heard the door open, so I turned off the TV and hit the nest. My mind was racing as Daniel and the dog crawled in to say "Hi." He kept wanting to put a band-aid on my boo boo. When they left, I drifted into sleep once more.

Chapter 11
Overwhelming Sadness

As my head cleared over the next two weeks, I knew it was wrong to let people think that I was dead or that Clayborn had killed me. I reasoned that I was doing the right thing, because the courts were not going to let Clayborn out with a murder charge against him. I feared Clayborn would go after my family. I managed to put it out of my thoughts and get on with the business of living in my nest. Daniel's mother stopped coming by and the community returned to normal.

Then Thursday morning I had gotten up and showered. I played on the computer and practiced the test taking material that was laying around. I fixed a grilled cheese for lunch and ate it with the news. I had taken a big bite out of an apple when the news person said that the father of the boy that had disappeared had been killed in a hit and run accident. The driver had been caught and had been drinking. Drink had at last killed my dad.

Suddenly, I was in tears. I couldn't get control. Just like that, the news went on to other things, but I was destroyed. I crawled into my nest and cried until I was so exhausted that I fell asleep.

I was cried out when I awoke in the middle of the night. I was confused but as I lay there, I tried to think more clearly. Dad had terrified me most of my childhood, with his yelling and threats. I had blamed him for every failure I had ever experienced. I couldn't remember a time when I could go to sleep without fear of his late night attacks. Yet, here I was, overwhelmingly sad. I didn't understand it. I guess he was my dad and a part of me. By morning I knew I had spent the last night in the safe haven of my nest. It broke my heart to leave. I longed to stay, but my mom needed me now. My sister needed me now. I didn't think beyond that.

When Bill and Judy left for work, I put on all my clothes, so I didn't have to carry anything. I had some juice, tea, and a bowl of cereal. I cleaned up everything. I wrapped my journal in foil, then I put it in a plastic bag. I sealed it with duct tape. I hid it under a big rock in the yard. Without looking back, I walked out the front door and down the street. I caught the early bus and sat back and closed my eyes.

I hurt inside and out. I felt like a toy that had been smashed. I exited the bus and made my way to the square. I sat down and just couldn't move.

I don't know how long I was there. All I know is at some point it began to rain. It was a steady, cold rain, but I didn't feel it. A cab driver stopped and talked to me. I could see his mouth moving, but I couldn't understand a word he said. Then there was a policeman and a life squad. I felt like I was watching a movie of someone else's life. I'm not sure what happened. There were doctors and nurses. There were policemen and social workers. At some point my mother came and sat by my bed. She smiled and talked kindly. I could tell she was kind, even though I couldn't understand a word she said.

I didn't know it at the time, but I had pneumonia, broken ribs, as well as many other injuries. After several days, I could sit up and eat. Mom and my sister were there and talked to me. Although I could hear and see, I could not understand language. I asked them for a pencil and paper. I asked my mom to write down what she was saying. That question resulted in more doctors and x-rays. The police came every day. I was glad I couldn't understand them. As the days passed, I slowly regained the ability to understand language. But I knew I WOULD NOT answer any questions about Clayborn Jackie. They kept saying that he was locked up, but I didn't trust them to keep him that way. I refused to answer any questions about where I had been. It was easy to do, because the doctors did not know that I could understand what they were saying. I prayed they would not find my journal. I guess it was smart to hide it, as long as no one found it. Every day the police would ask me where I had been. I would just look at them without speaking. Every day the police would ask me if Clayborn Jackie had hurt me. Again I would just look at them without speaking.

The police talked to the doctors and the doctors determined that I could have brain damage. They told the police to talk to me in six months. The doctors felt when my injuries healed, my problems might improve. Finally, I was allowed to go home with my mom. I was so glad to be back home. I thought it would be without fear, but it wasn't. Every night I woke up terrified. My heart would beat so fast that I thought it would explode. Mom said it would pass, but I was not so sure.

Chapter 12

Return to School

It was Monday and I was to be enrolled in school. My mom and I were in the office, and the school psychologist was talking to my mom while I sat on a chair outside the principal's office. My homeroom teacher was in there shouting at the principal. "That kid has been gone all year! Now he shows up the day before the state testing starts. He can't possibly pass. His scores will really hurt us. It's not fair!"

The principal said, "I'll suggest to the mom that he enroll

next week. She'll buy it. I'll tell her it is best for her son, that we don't want to put any more pressure on him. I wonder where he was. God knows what Jackie did to him. If Mom doesn't buy it, there isn't anything I can do about it. I'll put him back in your homeroom, since you had him at the beginning of the year. At least the paperwork says you had him in September."

"I know that is what the paperwork says, but I just don't remember him," my teacher said. "Now I am supposed to deal with possible brain damage? I doubt I can pull it off."

Mom came back and we were shown into the principal's office. The principal gave her the bit about me starting school next week. Suddenly I was really angry. I was tired of being invisible. I was tired of letting other people manipulate me. I stood up straight and looked the principal in the eye and said, "NO, I will be at school tomorrow. Testing is not too much pressure for me."

The teacher started one of those sentences that starts with a "But." I shot him a look and he shut up. The next day I was there with two number two pencils. Tuesday was Reading/Language Arts, Wednesday was Math, Thursday was Science, and Friday was Social

Studies. Just like that, testing was over. I didn't talk to anybody all week. No one talked to me. The kind neighbor lady, Mrs. Bea, baked me cookies and my sister and I loved them. She said I could come over and she would teach me how to bake them. She could see me. She always could. I WAS NOT INVISIBLE TO HER!

It was getting close to the end of the year. One day I was called to the principal's office. He had a pizza and a coke for me. He asked me to sit down and have lunch with him. I thought this was a very nice thing for him to do, but I wondered why? There had to be more to it. He could now see me. He remembered my name. There was more to it.

"We just got the test scores back," the principal said. "You made top scores in all subjects. Your math score was the highest we've ever had at this school. We are very proud of you. When you come to school next year, we will put you in our gifted classes. We have plans for you, young man."

I thanked him, but I didn't say much. When I left his office, the office workers smiled and gave me candy. They could see me too. When I went into my class, the teacher bragged on me and put down all the rest of the kids. Am I to believe that now he can see me? They glared at me. I didn't walk home after school. I walked to the square. I think better there. I sat still and put my thoughts in order.

1. The school had special classes for the gifted and the kids were treated nice.

2. The school had special classes for learning disabled and physically handicapped, and the kids were treated nice.

3. The kids who play sports got treated nice.

4. The largest part of the class were just average good people, and they were ignored.

All of these things I knew to be true. But I had the feeling that the system wouldn't be so nice to these groups unless there was something else involved, like money.

Every day now, the psychologist would call me in for a chat. Was I happy, did I have what I need, was there anything I wanted to talk about? He always seemed a little sad when I said there wasn't. He seemed like a nice enough person. I decided to ask the big question.

"Does someone get money if they have kids in special education or the gifted program?" I asked.

He looked hard at me, as if he was thinking. "Well, no one person gets money, but the school gets funding for those programs. Some of the money comes from the federal government. And if the school testing is poor year after year, schools lose students and teachers, so of course we want to do well. Why are you asking these questions? With your scores you don't have anything to worry about."

"I just wanted the average kids to be treated nice, I guess," I said. "I've been treated really nice, since I got good scores. If my scores are bad next year, will I be treated bad again?"

"If your scores were bad, we would wonder why, and look for ways to raise them. I understand what you are asking though. Funding for a special group must be spent on that group. You're saying that you would like it if all students were treated as though they were special. Did someone in this school treat you badly?"

"I didn't mean bad like hitting. I meant average kids don't get the extra field trips or rewards like the others."

"You know you have been through a lot of horrible stuff. It will take a while to work through it. You must be careful that you don't let what happened to you make you a bitter person. Don't give up accepting kindness and trusting others because of your experience. Does that make sense to you?"

It did make sense to me. I was letting what happened to me cloud my life. I didn't trust the principal, the teacher, or the kids for that matter; I didn't trust my mom all that much. I was angry all the time. I guess I knew that my school success was because I was hiding and bored. Studying gave me something to do. I could feel good about it and it became like a game. I didn't want to give that up. I didn't want to sit at school and feel angry all day. Slowly a plan took place in my head. The next day I ran it by the psychologist.

"What do you think of me staying home next year and doing home schooling?" I asked.

"Are you afraid of coming to school?" he asked.

"No," I said. "I am not afraid. It's just I can learn better and faster on my own."

"I don't think the home schooling is a bad idea," he continued, "it's just I hate to see you isolate yourself from other kids your age."

"Isn't there a way to do it without isolating myself?" I asked.

"Well, if you had after school activities with others it might be okay," he said.

I did a lot of searching on the computer at the library that night and found two schools in my state that would send me everything I needed. They'd send books, computers, science stuff, all of it. I had no doubt that I could do it. I had proven I could do it. It was the social activities that worried me. I decided to ask around.

I found out that there was a church where kids go one night a week. They have a program where they feed you, you learn some Bible stuff, and then they play games. If you're my age, you can play basketball. I could take my sister too. She needed some fun. There is a group of policemen that work with boys my age and teach them camping, swimming, and stuff like that. I didn't have to be bad, handicapped, or anything to join. The guy from the Middle East that owned the store said I could work for him a couple of hours each day. I could shovel snow, sweep up, take out the trash, and stock shelves. I could do it in the daytime if I'm home-schooled. I got excited just thinking about it.

My mom, the psychologist, the principal, my teacher, and I sat down for a talk. Everyone but the psychologist thought I was making a mistake. I didn't care what they thought because I was going to make it happen with or without them. I didn't say that though. I acted like I really cared what they thought. The psychologist said he thought that maybe I needed to be home-schooled to adjust to all that had happened. He told me privately that I might consider going to a regular high school when the time came. I told him I just might like that. After much discussion, I just said very clearly, "I am going to be home-schooled next year, and that is the end of it. I will agree to state tests at the end of the year." Everyone got quiet and the meeting ended.

The police came to talk to me. Six months had passed. They told me that the boys with Clayborn Jackie had squealed about another murder Jackie had done. So he was still held for murder.

They didn't need my testimony, although they wanted me to talk. I just couldn't do it. I couldn't trust enough to do it. They said they wished me well and left.

Mom had a little more money now that Dad didn't take it. We had food in the house and we fixed the place up a little. My sister wouldn't let me out of her sight. I became the cook. Every night I would have dinner on the table when Mom came home. Home was a peaceful place now.

One weekend I rode the bus with my sister to Milford to get my journal out from under the rock. I took her to Skyline for chili and bought her a doll from the thrift store. I wanted to share that part of my life with her. I didn't tell her I had lived there. I just said it was a nice place to visit. We walked to 60 Mound Street and I carefully got my journal from beneath the rock. We walked up the street a block or two and saw Judy carrying the dog Penny home. "Hi," I said to her. I had always wanted to talk to her.

"How are you doing?" she said. "I haven't seen you around lately."

She had never seen me before, but I didn't say anything.

"I don't live in Milford anymore," I said. "How is your grandson?" I inquired. I missed the dog and Daniel.

"He is going to have his third birthday soon. He is so cute. He said his pretend friend moved away. I wonder how he thinks that stuff up," she said.

I knew it! Daniel did see me, so did Bill, so did Penny, and so did Judy. I think, maybe, I'll live in Milford some day. My sister and I caught the bus home, but I knew I'd be back.

ABOUT THE AUTHOR

Judith Toombs Gatch was an inner city public special education teacher who is now retired. Her imagination and her creative spin take us on this young boy's journey of self-discovery. Judy's husband said to her one day, "You know, somebody could live in our basement and we'd never know it because of all this junk." This remark was the spark for this story. As older family members passed on, Judy accumulated their belongings to sort and store in her basement – perfect for nest-building. Judy lives in Milford, Ohio where the junk still remains; it's just arranged differently now and again!

Made in the USA
Columbia, SC
22 February 2022